Benjamin Rabbit

and the

Story by Irene Keller

Illustrations by Dick Keller

Dodd, Mead & Company

New York

Stranger Danger

Distributed in Canada by McClelland and Stewart Limited, Toronto
Manufactured in the United States of America
1   2   3   4   5   6   7   8   9   10

Library of Congress Cataloging in Publication Data

Keller, Irene.
   Benjamin Rabbit and the stranger danger.

   Summary: Benjamin learns what to do when strangers pay attention to him.
   1. Children's stories, American. [1. Safety — Fiction.
2. Strangers — Fiction.   3. Rabbits — Fiction]   I. Keller,
Dick, ill. II. Title.
PZ7.K28133Be   1985   [E]   84-28673
ISBN 0-396-08655-1

Benjamin Rabbit hopped across the puddles on his way to school. Small as he was, Benjamin was a first-rate puddle jumper. And, young as he was, Benjamin knew a lot.

For one thing, Benjamin knew his full name. His first
name—Benjamin—and his last name—Rabbit. And he
knew his mother's name—Maud—and his father's name
—Claude.

Benjamin also knew his phone number *and* his area code—TEN numbers! He knew them by heart.

And he knew his address—46 Green Street in the town of Meadowbank in the state of Ohio.

His teacher said it was important to know the name of the town and the name of the state where you live.

Benjamin liked his teacher a lot. She helped him learn to read and write. And sometimes she invited other people to come to school and talk to the students. Special people—like fire fighters and police officers.

That very morning, when Benjamin got to school, a police officer named Sergeant Strong came in to talk to Benjamin and his classmates.

Sergeant Strong began by saying that he had some very bad news. He told the class that Katy Cottontail had disappeared! And she was last seen talking to a stranger.

Benjamin could hardly believe it. He was very upset. He felt like crying.

"I know it's sad," said Sergeant Strong. "And I know it's scary. But we're going to talk about Stranger Danger —bad strangers. You need to know how you can make sure it won't happen to *you*."

Benjamin sat up straight and paid attention.

"First," said Sergeant Strong, "does everyone know what a stranger is?"

"I do," said Benjamin. "A stranger is a grown-up you don't know."

"Right," said Sergeant Strong. "But how can we tell a good stranger from a bad stranger?"

"I guess we can't," said Benjamin.

"Right," said Sergeant Strong. "That's why we have to be careful of *all* strangers. Bad strangers and good strangers can look alike.

"Now I'm going to give you a list of Stranger Danger Do's and Don'ts. We will read it out loud."

STRANGER DANGER DO'S AND DON'TS

1. **DON'T** Talk to Strangers.

2. **DON'T** Go Near a Stranger's Car.

3. **DON'T** Take Candy or Money or Anything Else from a Stranger.

If a stranger follows you by car or on foot,

4. **DO** Yell "Help!" as Loud as You Can.

5. **DO** Run to the Nearest Place Where There Are Other People.

6. **DON'T** Run to a Lonely Place.

If you are home alone,

7. **DON'T** Open the Door for Anyone.

8. **DON'T** Tell Anyone on the Phone That You Are Home Alone.

DO

DON'T

"Now," said Sergeant Strong. "Let's pretend for a moment. I want you to imagine that you are out shopping in a store and all of a sudden you don't see your mother anywhere. You're lost! OK?"

Benjamin nodded, "OK."

"What would you do?" asked Sergeant Strong. "Would you ask a stranger to help you find your mother?"

"No!" yelled the class.

"Would you go to the parking lot to look for your mother?"

"No!" yelled the class.

"Would you go to the nearest check-out counter and ask the check-out person to help you find your mother?"

"Yes!" yelled the class.

"Right," said Sergeant Strong. "If you are lost in a store or a shopping mall, you go to the nearest check-out counter and ask the clerk to help you."

"I can do that," said Benjamin.

"Of course you can," said Sergeant Strong. "Now let's pretend again. Imagine you're home alone. Your mother is not home."

Benjamin nodded.

"Suppose the doorbell rings or someone knocks on the door," said Sergeant Strong. "Would you open the door?"

"No!" yelled the class.

"Right," said Sergeant Strong. "Never open the door to anyone when you are home alone.

"But what if the phone rings and someone asks to speak to your mother. Do you say, 'My mother's not home'?"

"No!" yelled the class.

"Right," said Sergeant Strong. "But what *would* you say if someone on the phone asks to speak to your mother?"

"I know," said Benjamin. "I'd say, 'My mother's busy and she can't come to the phone.' And then I'd hang up right away."

"Very good," said Sergeant Strong. "Never tell anyone on the phone that you're home alone."

"I see you know a lot," the sergeant went on. "And now I'm going to tell you some Stranger Danger tricks. You've all been taught to be kind and helpful to other people, right?"

"Right," said Benjamin.

"So what do you do if a stranger asks for your help?" Benjamin Rabbit didn't know.

"What if you are out playing," said Sergeant Strong,
"and a stranger says, 'I hurt my arm. Will you help me
carry this package?'

"Or suppose a stranger says, 'Help me open my car
door. It's stuck. You're so strong, I bet you could open it.'

"Would you help that stranger?"

"No!" yelled the class.

"Right," said Sergeant Strong. "Good strangers don't ask youngsters to help them. They ask other grown-ups. NEVER talk to strangers! And if a stranger talks to you, ignore it. Pretend you don't hear it and walk away."

"I can do that," said Benjamin.

Benjamin hurried home from school that day to tell his mother all he had learned. He had hopped about halfway home—with a lot of lovely puddles still to cross —when he suddenly noticed that a car was coasting along beside him, very slowly, next to the curb.

"Hi!" he heard a voice say. "You're getting wet. Hop in. I'll give you a ride."

Benjamin pretended not to hear. He hopped a little faster.

"Your mother sent me to get you," said the stranger. "She's sick and she sent me to bring you home."

Benjamin knew that was a Stranger Danger trick. His mother would never send a stranger to get him. He hopped as far from the curb as he could get.

"OK, pal," said the stranger. "I bet you don't know so much. I bet you don't even know the way to Main Street."

"I bet I *do* know," said Benjamin. "It's two blocks over."

"What? What did you say?" said the stranger, opening the car door. "I can't hear you. Come a little closer."

Benjamin started to move toward the car and then—just in time—he remembered the Stranger Danger Do's and Don'ts. DON'T GO NEAR A STRANGER'S CAR!

Benjamin ran like the wind, yelling, "Help!" as loud as he could. When he got to the corner, he told the crossing guard about the bad stranger.

When he got home, he told his mother.

"You did the right things, Benjamin," said his mother, giving him an extra-big hug. "I'm so glad you know the Stranger Danger Do's and Don'ts. Always remember them."

Benjamin put the list on his wall where he would see it every day. And Benjamin Rabbit always remembered. Yes, Benjamin Rabbit knew a lot.